melville house classics

THE DUEL

THE DUEL

HEINRICH
VON KLEIST

TRANSLATED BY ANNIE JANUSCH

MELVILLEHOUSE
BROOKLYN, NEW YORK

THE DUEL BY HEINRICH VON KLEIST

ORIGINALLY PUBLISHED IN GERMAN AS *DER ZWEIKAMPF*
IN THE COLLECTION *ERZHÄLUNGEN* IN 1810

TRANSLATION © 2011 BY ANNIE JANUSCH
© 2011 MELVILLE HOUSE PUBLISHING

FIRST MELVILLE HOUSE PRINTING: JUNE 2011

MELVILLE HOUSE PUBLISHING
145 PLYMOUTH STREET
BROOKLYN, NY 11201

WWW.MHPBOOKS.COM

ISBN: 978-1-935554-53-0

BOOK DESIGN: CHRISTOPHER KING, BASED ON
A SERIES DESIGN BY DAVID KONOPKA

PRINTED IN THE UNITED STATES OF AMERICA

1 2 3 4 5 6 7 8 9 10

   LIBRARY OF CONGRESS CATALOGING-IN-PUBLICATION DATA

KLEIST, HEINRICH VON, 1777-1811.
  [ZWEIKAMPF. ENGLISH]
THE DUEL / HEINRICH VON KLEIST ; TRANSLATED BY ANNIE JANUSCH.
    P. CM.
  ISBN 978-1-935554-53-0
I. JANUSCH, ANNIE. II. TITLE.
PT2378.Z913 2011
838'.609--DC23
                          2011021336

THE DUEL

Toward the end of the fourteenth century, as night was falling on the feastday of St. Remigius, Duke Wilhelm von Breysach—who had been living in enmity with his half-brother, Count Jakob Rotbart, ever since the Duke's clandestine marriage to a countess reputedly below his social rank, Katharina von Heersbruck of the family Alt-Hüningen—returned from a meeting with the German Kaiser in Worms, at which the Duke had persuaded the Kaiser to legitimize as his one natural son, Count Philip von Hüningen, who had been conceived before marriage, the Duke's other children born in wedlock having died. Envisioning what the future now held, the Duke felt more content than he had during the entire course of his reign, but just as he reached the park behind his castle, an arrow shot out suddenly from the darkness of the hedges, drilling through his body until it lodged tightly beneath his breastbone. Seized by this event, Sir Friedrich von Trota, the Duke's chamberlain, carried him with the help of the other knights into the castle, where an assembly of the Reich's vassals was called by the Duke's distraught wife, and there in her arms the Duke gathered his remaining strength to deliver a final address in which he set forth the Kaiser's decree. It was not without lively opposition, however, that the vassals carried out the Duke's last authoritative will, as the rule of law would have called for his half-brother, Count Jakob Rotbart, to reap the crown. After furnishing the Kaiser's consent, and on the condition that the Duke's wife be appointed guardian and regent until the young prince came of age, Count Philip was indeed recognized as heir to the throne—and the Duke lay back and died.

And so the Duchess ascended the throne, quite without ceremony, and sent but an envoy to notify her brother-in-law, Count Jakob Rotbart, of the throne's new heir. What several knights of the court conjectured would happen—believing they'd cracked the

Count's impervious demeanor—happened, or so it seemed: Count Jakob Rotbart, in cunning assessment of this news, rose above the injustice done him by his brother, or, at least he refrained from contesting the Duke's last will, and instead offered his congratulations to his nephew on the throne he had acquired. Rotbart gathered the members of the Duchess's envoy congenially to his table and regaled them with how he had lived freely and independently in his castle since the death of his wife, who had left him a kingly sum; how he delighted in the company of his neighboring noblemen's wives as well as wine from his own vineyards and a jaunty hunt with friends; and how he planned a crusade to the Holy Land to atone for the sins of an impetuous youth (alas, his trespasses only increased with age, he conceded), which would be the last endeavor he looked forward to at the end of his life.

Rotbart's ambivalence toward the throne sparked bitter rebuke from his two sons, who, having been brought up with their own aspirations to succession, now found their hopes unexpectedly dashed. Rotbart gave the insolent youths a terse and derisive reprimand, ordering them to accompany him into the town for the occasion of their uncle's funeral and to stand at his side while the Duke was laid to rest in the family vault. After the Count had paid his respects to his nephew, the young prince—in the throne room of the castle, and in the presence of the duchess and the court's other dignitaries—he returned to his castle, having declined the duchess's offers of offices and honors, and accompanied by the blessings of the people, who revered him now all the more for his show of graciousness and temperance.

With her first obligation as regent having reached an unexpectedly tidy end, the Duchess now turned her attention toward the pressing task of finding her husband's murderers—whole packs of them, it was rumored, had been seen in the park. She and her Chancellor, Sir Godwin von Herrthal, began their investigation by examining the fatal arrow, which revealed nothing as to the identity of its owner except perhaps for its unusually exquisite craftsmanship. Crisp and brilliantly rippling feathers were tucked into a slender yet sturdy shaft that was finely worked from dark walnut. The arrowhead was clad in gleaming brass; only the very point, sharp as a fishbone, was of steel. It appeared to have been manufactured for the armory of a wealthy aristocrat, who either was embroiled in frequent feuds or was an avid hunter. Since the date engraved on the arrowhead indicated its recent manufacture, however, the Duchess, at the Chancellor's advice, sent the arrow under the crown seal to all the workshops in Germany, in order to discover the arrowsmith who had made it, and once found, to learn the name of the patron who had commissioned the fatal arrow.

Five months passed before written word arrived from an arrowsmith in Strasbourg, testifying that he had made three-score such arrows, as well as a quiver to hold them, just three years earlier for Count Jakob Rotbart. Sir Godwin, whom the Duchess had since placed in charge of the investigation, was most alarmed by this message and kept it locked away for several weeks. Despite Rotbart's openly debaucherous life, he was still, in Sir Godwin's estimation, too noble-minded to be capable of such an abhorrent deed as murdering his own brother. Despite the Duchess's many exemplary qualities, her sense of justice in a matter implicating the life of her husband's most bitter foe led Sir Godwin to believe he should proceed with utmost caution. He decided to pursue this peculiar lead in the investigation discreetly. However, when he learned by chance from city officials that Rotbart—who nearly never, or seldom at best, left his castle—had been gone the night of the Duke's murder, he considered it his duty to disclose his findings and to brief the Duchess in detail at the next council meeting on the charges that now threw strange and surprising suspicion on her brother-in-law, Count Jakob Rotbart.

The Duchess, however, was quite pleased with herself for having come to such amicable terms with her brother-in-law, and she feared nothing more than to provoke him with any imprudent action. To Sir Godwin's consternation, the Duchess gave not the slightest sign of joy at these dubious findings, but rather, after carefully reading the documents through twice, expressed grave displeasure that such a delicate and irresolute matter should be brought up publicly before the council. Convinced that the information was false or libelous, the Duchess prohibited it from being brought before the court. Indeed, even Sir Godwin's mere mention before the council struck her as a risk in light of the exceptional, nearly fanatical, popularity that her brother-in-law had consequently enjoyed since being refused the throne. In order to intercept any rumors that might reach his ears, the Duchess sent her brother-in-law a judiciously written letter, outlining the accusations implicating him in his brother's murder along with the alleged evidence—and dismissing them as outlandish misunderstandings, with no uncertain request that he spare her any denial of his innocence in order to preserve her opinion of him.

Rotbart was seated among friends at his own table when a knight entered, bearing the Duchess's letter. He politely stood up, taking the letter over to the arch of a window to read, while his friends studied the solemn messenger who declined to be seated. Rotbart had barely glanced through the letter, however, when he turned to his friends, his face suddenly flush: "Brothers, look at what a shameful accusation has been brought against me in my brother's murder!" Rotbart seized the arrow from the knight's hand with a seething glare, his friends crowding anxiously around. Then, hiding his devastation, he conceded that the arrow did indeed belong to him and that he had in fact been away from his castle on the night of St. Remigius. His friends railed against such fierce and pernicious duplicity, slinging the suspicion of murder back at the Duchess, and just as they were on the verge of turning their rancor onto the messenger for having risen to his Duchess's defense, Rotbart intervened. Having read the letter now more carefully, he called out, "Hold on, my friends!" and, retrieving his sword from the corner of the room, he surrendered it to the knight with the words, "I am your prisoner." Puzzled, the knight asked whether he had heard correctly, and whether he acknowledged the two charges drawn up by the Chancellor, to which Rotbart replied three times, "Yes!" He added, however, that he hoped it would be unnecessary for him to prove his innocence unless before a court formally convened by the Duchess. Dismayed, his own knights pleaded in vain that under such circumstances he needn't be held accountable to anyone but the Kaiser himself. But Rotbart was resolute in his thinking and insisted on appealing to the Duchess's sense of justice by appearing before her tribunal. Tearing himself free, he shouted out the window for his horse—prepared, as he said, to follow the Duchess's knight into immediate custody—when his own knights forcibly intervened with one condition Rotbart was willing to accept. They set to writing to the Duchess, offering a bail of twenty-thousand silver marks with the assurance that Rotbart would stand before her assembled tribunal and comply with its verdict in exchange for the safe conduct to which every knight is entitled.

Baffled by the knights' petition, and with heinous rumors already circulating about her motives concerning her brother-in-law, the Duchess thought it wise to recuse herself entirely from the matter and submit it instead to the Kaiser's court. On the advice of her Chancellor, she gathered all the documents pertaining to the case and solicited him, in his propriety as Kaiser, to relieve her of an investigation in which she herself was an interested party. The Kaiser, who was in Basel at the time for negotiations with the Swiss Confederation, approved the Duchess's request, appointing a court of three counts, twelve knights, and two assistant judges. Granting Rotbart safe conduct for a bail set at twenty-thousand silver marks in compliance with his knights' petition, he summoned him to appear before the assembled court and to respond to the two charges brought against him: how an arrow, which, by his own confession, belonged to him, should have fallen into the hands of his brother's murderer; and where he had passed the night of St. Remigius, if not at his own castle.

On the Monday after Trinity, Count Jakob Rotbart appeared with an exquisite escort of knights before the court. Waiving the first charge, which he conceded he was at a loss to explain, he proceeded to the second and crucial point of contention: "Gentlemen," he began, resting his hands on the banister and looking out at the assembly from small, sprightly eyes, veiled by red lashes. "You accuse me—I, who have demonstrated ample proof of my indifference to crown and scepter—of the most heinous deed that can be perpetrated: the murder of my brother, who, for all our animosity, was no less dear to me. Your accusation is based in part on the grounds that I happened to be away from my castle for the first time in several years on the night of St. Remigius. Now, I know very well that a knight must dutifully protect the honor of a lady whose favor he discreetly enjoys, and truly, had the heavens not suspended this strange fate above my head, this secret, which sleeps in my heart, would have died with me, turned to dust—and only when the last angel's trumpet blasts open our graves would it rise with me to stand before God. As you yourselves probably realize, however, these considerations are rendered void by the question now laid at my conscience by the Kaiser's majesty as vested in this court. Alas, if you must know why it's neither probable nor even possible for me to have had any hand—personally, or indirectly—in my brother's murder, then I'm left with little choice but to disclose that on the night of St. Remigius, at that very hour when the murder was committed, I was secretly paying visit to Lord Winfried von Breda's beautiful daughter, Lady Littegarde von Auerstein, whose ardent assent I had at last won."

Now, it is important to add that Lady Littegarde von Auerstein was not only widely regarded as the most beautiful of women but also—until this ignominious moment—as the most fair and immaculate by reputation. She had led a quiet and reclusive life in her father's castle ever since the death of her husband, whom she had lost to an infectious fever just months after their marriage. Only at the prompting of her aging father, who wished to see her remarried, Littegarde consented to appear occasionally at the hunts and banquets attended by the knights from the surrounding areas, and in particular, by Count Jakob

Rotbart. Lords of the highest nobility and wealth would pay court to Littegarde at every opportunity. Her most cherished among them, though, was none other than Sir Friedrich von Trota, the late Duke Wilhelm von Breysach's chamberlain, who had once bravely saved Littegarde from the path of a wounded, charging boar. Despite her father's admonishments, Littegarde had wavered in giving Sir Friedrich her hand in marriage, out of fear that her two brothers would disapprove, as they were dependent on her inheritance. Indeed, when Rudolph, her eldest brother, married a wealthy young woman from a neighboring area, who, to the great joy of the family, bore him an heir after three childless years, Littegarde was pressed by her brothers to preserve the unity of their family. And so she bid formal farewell to Friedrich in a letter written amid profuse tears, and agreed to become an abbess in a convent not far from her father's castle on the banks of the Rhine.

It was just as Littegarde's plans were pending under the Archbishop of Strasbourg's review that her father received word from the Kaiser's appointed court, informing him of the allegation disgracing his daughter and summoning her to appear in Basel in order to respond to the charge brought against her by Count Jakob Rotbart. Detailed in the letter were the exact hour and place, at which Rotbart, according to his testimony, claimed to have paid his clandestine visit. Enclosed, too, was a ring belonging to Littegarde's late husband, which Rotbart claimed to have been given upon their parting as a token by which to remember his night with her.

Littegarde's elderly father had been in poor health, suffering from an ailment that was quite serious at his age and caused him great discomfort. Moving unsteadily about the room on his daughter's arm, while inwardly already reckoning his declining days, the arrival of the court's letter found him at a fragile moment—and gripped by its devastating news, he collapsed in a stroke, the pages of the letter falling to the floor around him. While Littegarde's brothers heaved their father up from the floor, calling for a doctor and attempting to resuscitate him—and Littegarde, having fainted, lay in the arms of her maids— their father surrendered his soul. Alas, Littegarde was not permitted even the bittersweet consolation of a final imparted word that would affirm her honor and accompany her father into eternity.

Littegarde's brothers reeled from the shock of their father's sudden death, appalled and furious that their sister's shameful behavior should have played a part in it. The letter's evidence was too condemning to disbelieve, for they knew all too well that Count Jakob Rotbart had paid adamant court to Littegarde the previous summer, going so far as to hold several tournaments and banquets in her honor, at which he had been improperly attentive to her. Her brothers now recalled that right around the time of St. Remigius, Littegarde's ring from her late husband happened to have gone missing—supposedly while she was out for a walk—only to now curiously turn up in the hands of Rotbart, thus leaving few doubts as to the veracity of Rotbart's testimony. As their father's body was taken away by the castle's grieving servants, Littegarde clung to her brothers' knees, pleading with them to listen to her for just one moment. Rudolph asked indignantly whether she might produce a witness who could reasonably dispute the accusation. Trembling, Littegarde responded that she could summon only her own irreproachable character, as her chambermaid, having been granted leave to visit her parents, had not attended to Littegarde on the night in question. Livid, Rudolph shrugged her off with a kick, and, unsheathing his sword and calling for his servants, commanded her to leave their home and castle that instant. Littegard, pale as chalk, got up from the floor, and, silently withstanding his abuse, begged him to at least allow her a bit of time to make the necessary arrangements, but Rudolph only seethed with rage, shouting, "Out! Get out!" His own wife attempted to intervene, pleading with him to calm down and show his sister a little mercy, to which Rudolph responded by flinging his wife aside with the hilt of his sword, so forcefully that the blow drew blood. And so Littegarde departed, a poor wretch who felt more dead than alive. People stood around her, staring as she stumbled across the courtyard to the castle gates, where she was handed a bundle of clothing in which a bit of money had been stowed. Cursing his sister's name, Rudolph sealed the gates behind her.

This sudden plunge from the heights of serene felicity to the depths of unfathomable distress was more than poor Littegarde could bear. She set out, not knowing where to turn but in search of a place to sleep for the night, and staggered down the stone path, clinging to its railing for support. Before she had even reached the small village strewn in the valley below, Littegarde sank to the earth, robbed of all strength, a deep sleep insulating her from her suffering. The cover of darkness was almost complete when she awoke nearly a full hour later encircled by several concerned villagers. A boy playing on the hillside nearby had caught sight of this curious woman and run and told his parents, who were aghast to discover that woman to be Littegarde, whose past charity they now eagerly reciprocated. She was brought to senses all too harshly, however, by the sight of her father's castle in the distance, and, declining all offers to be taken back there, Littegarde asked only for the courtesy of a guide for her journey forth. Despite their best efforts, the villagers could not persuade her that she was unfit for travel. Littegarde truly believed it perilous to remain a moment longer within her brothers' precinct, and with the crowd of concerned onlookers only growing, she sought to force her way through their ranks and set off alone. With night falling, and fearing that they might be held responsible by the castle's lordship should any misfortune befall Littegarde, the villagers finally granted her request and arranged for a carriage to drive her, after much prodding as to her destination, to Basel.

Once underway, though, Littegarde reevaluated the situation facing her in Basel, and she instructed the driver to turn the carriage around and redirect it to Sir Friedrich von Trota's castle, which lay not too far away. She was quite certain that without formidable defense she could not succeed against an opponent like Rotbart before the court in Basel, and she could entrust no one more worthy or noble with the task of defending her honor than her still devoted friend Friedrich. Though it must have been nearly midnight when Littegarde arrived with her carriage, thoroughly exhausted from the trip, the castle lights still shone. A servant came out to greet her carriage and was sent back up to announce her arrival, but he was happily intercepted by Friedrich's two sisters, Bertha and Kunigunde, who had been attending to a household matter in the front hall. All too delighted to greet their old friend Littegarde, they helped her down from her carriage, and led her—albeit, not without trepidation—to their brother, who was seated at his desk, besieged by documents from a lawsuit. Hearing the sound of their approach, Friedrich turned, astonished to find Littegarde—pale and mussed, a picture of despair—falling to her knees before him. "My dear Littegarde," he cried, lifting her up from the floor. "What's happened?" Littegarde lowered herself onto a chair and told Friedrich all that had transpired: how Count Jakob Rotbart had brought a despicable accusation against her before the court in Basel just to clear himself of suspicion in his brother's murder; how the news of it had caused her father's stroke, and how he had passed away just moments later in her brothers' arms; and how, without even being afforded the chance to defend herself, she had been reproached with uncommon abuse by her own brothers and chased like a criminal from her home. Littegarde asked whether Friedrich might recommend a lawyer in Basel who could offer her prudent counsel in refuting Rotbart's shameful allegation before the Kaiser's appointed court. Littegarde assured him that had such words escaped the mouth of a Parthian or Persian, whom she had never laid eyes on, it could not have shocked her more than coming from Rotbart, whom she profoundly despised—as much for his swaggering reputation as for his swarthy looks. At the previous summer's banquets, she had coolly and persistently spurned every compliment that he had taken the liberty of paying her. "Enough, my dear Littegarde!" Friedrich said, taking her hand and pressing it to his lips with ardent gallantry. "Don't waste another word justifying your innocence! In my heart speaks a voice whose resonance and conviction are greater than any of your assurances—indeed, greater than all the evidence and legal grounds capable of being construed before the court in Basel. Since your own brothers have shown themselves to be dishonorable, take me as your brother and friend, and permit me the glory of advocating on your behalf. I will restore the resplendence of your name before the judgment of the court—and before the judgment of the whole world!" Littegarde could not contain her gracious tears at such a noble pledge, and she allowed Friedrich to present her as a guest to his mother, on the pretext that a family dispute had prompted her to take leave in the Trota castle. Although Friedrich's mother had already retired to her chamber for the night, she attended to Littegarde with particular affection, calling for an entire wing of the spacious castle to be appointed that very night, replete with clothing and linens from Friedrich's sisters' own wardrobes, and allocating a considerable staff to her service. Just three days later found Sir Friedrich von Trota on the road to Basel with an impressive entourage of knights and squires, but without having revealed how he planned to prove Littegarde's innocence before Rotbart and the court.

In the meantime, a letter from Littegarde's brothers had arrived in Basel, in which they recounted the recent events at their father's castle, and—because they either sincerely believed her to be guilty, or else possessed other motives for her undoing—cast their sister as a proven criminal, deserving of the full severity of the law. They even ventured so falsely as to describe her banishment from the castle as a "voluntary fleeing," after she had been unable to offer any adequate proof of her innocence. Admittedly, they had perhaps expressed some brotherly indignation, but, they swore, having since undertaken a concerned and thorough search for her whereabouts to no avail, they could only presume that their sister now traipsed the land with some rogue consort, serving out her sentence of disgrace. Furthermore, Littegarde's brothers petitioned the court to have her name struck from the family tree in order to redeem their good name, and for her claims to their noble father's estate to be forfeited, as fit punishment for having driven him to his grave with her shamefulness.

Now, the judges in Basel were not subject to rule on the brothers' petition, as the matter fell squarely outside their jurisdiction. However, that Rotbart had since dispatched his own knights to search out Littegarde—even offering refuge at his castle—struck the court as the most indicting and conclusive proof yet as to the truth of his testimony, and thus proceeded to dismiss the charges brought against him in his brother's murder. Indeed, the selfless charity Rotbart displayed toward Littegarde at her fallen hour overwhelmingly restored the public's faith in him— the trial in Basel having cost him a bit of fellowship recently. After all, divulging a good woman's name in an unscrupulous love affair was considered contemptible. However, in light of the extraordinary circumstances in which Rotbart's own life and honor were at stake, it was now widely recognized that he had had little alternative but to reveal in full his indecent alibi from the night of St. Remigius.

Rotbart was summoned before the Kaiser's court one last time for a public acquittal to clear him of all suspicion in the case of his brother's murder. In the halls of the venerable court, the herald read aloud the letter from Littegarde's brothers, and just as the judges were preparing their exonerating statement of the accused man, Sir Friedrich von Trota asked to approach the bench and inspect the letter for himself, as was customarily permitted every spectator. With the eyes of all the court upon him, Sir Friedrich snapped the letter from the herald's outstretched hands, and, giving it a cursory look, proceeded to tear the letter from top to bottom. He rolled the pieces neatly into his glove, and, pronouncing Rotbart a vile slanderer, threw the glove into Rotbart's face—challenging him to a trial by combat to settle once and for all the question of Littegarde's innocence before the eyes of God and the world. Pale, Rotbart picked up the gauntlet, saying: "As certain as God's judgment is just, so will I resolutely prove in an honest knight's duel the truthfulness of what I was forced to divulge about the Lady Littegarde. Gentlemen!" he continued, turning to the assembly of judges, "Inform the Kaiser of Sir Friedrich's court intrusion and request him to appoint the time and place where we may settle this dispute with swords in hand." With that, the court was adjourned and an envoy was dispatched to the Kaiser. Sir Friedrich's stepping forth to defend Littegarde did indeed shake the Kaiser's faith in Rotbart's testimony, and so, as custom dictated, and in order to settle the unusual circumstances surrounding this dispute, the Kaiser summoned Lady Littegarde to Basel as a witness, and appointed the feastday of St. Margaret and the Basel castle square as the time and place where Sir Friedrich von Trota and Count Jakob Rotbart would meet in Lady Littegarde's presence.

The midday sun of St. Margaret's Day was just rising above Basel's city towers, and an immense crowd of people was gathering in the castle square where benches and platforms had been erected to seat spectators, when, at the herald's trumpeted call, the two armored knights, Sir Friedrich and Count Jakob Rotbart, stepped onto the field before the judges' stand. Nearly the entire knighthood from Swabia and Switzerland had assembled on the slope leading up to the castle, and the Kaiser had taken his place on the balcony, joined by his wife and his sons and daughters, the princes and princesses. Just before the duel was set to begin, while the judges situated the opponents on the field, dividing the midday sun and shade equitably between them, Friedrich's mother, Helena, and his two sisters, Bertha and Kunigunde, who had accompanied Littegarde to Basel, approached the guards at the gates of the square for permission to speak with the lady, who, in accordance with longstanding custom, was seated on a platform on the battlefield itself. Although Helena and her daughters knew Littegarde to be a righteous and trustworthy woman, they could not deny their misgivings about the coincidence of her late husband's ring falling into Rotbart's possession, nor her chambermaid having been away on the one night she was now most needed to have served as witness. They resolved to test her one last time by reminding her just how senseless, indeed blasphemous, it would be for her to go through with this duel—its divine verdict and irrevocable repercussions—should even a modicum of guilt weigh on her conscience at this critical hour. Littegarde had good reason to contemplate the courageous step Friedrich was prepared to take for her—the gallows awaited them both should God deliver his infallible verdict in Rotbart's favor. At the sight of Friedrich's mother and sisters, Littegarde rose from her seat with a characteristic air of dignity, made all the more poignant by her recent suffering, and asked what brought them to her at such a dire moment. "My dear daughter," said Helena, taking her aside, "please understand, my son is my only consolation in this old age—spare me the heartache of having to mourn him at his grave. Before this duel should even get underway, we could put you in a carriage and take you to one of our properties across the Rhine, where you would be received without judgment and modestly looked after—as a gift from us."

Littegarde was silent a moment as she comprehended the implication of this offer, then bowed to one knee before Helena, a paleness overtaking her countenance. "Madame, with all respect," she said, "is it the heart of your noble son which now fears for my soul's innocence here on this field and before God's judgment?"

"Why do you ask?" asked Helena.

"Should the hand that wields his sword have any doubts, then I implore your son to abandon the field at once to his opponent and leave my soul's fate to God's own pitiless hand."

"No," said Helena, "my son knows nothing of this—he would never be so audacious as to defend you in the courtroom only to turn around and beg you to reconsider at this crucial hour. Friedrich stands in steadfast belief of your innocence, as you can see, armored and prepared to fight the man who insulted your honor. It was my daughters and I who, in a faltering moment of worry, thought of this—we meant only to avoid any misfortunes."

"Well, then," said Littegarde, her tears wetting the old woman's hand as she placed a kiss upon it, "let your son keep his word. No guilt inhabits my conscience—even if he were to go into battle without helmet and armor, God and all his angels would protect him!" Littegarde stood back up and led Helena and her daughters over to where seats had been placed behind her own crimson-covered chair on the stand.

At a nod from the Kaiser, the herald sounded his trumpet for the duel to commence, and the two knights, swords and shields in hand, advanced. Though his sword was not particularly long, Friedrich surprised Rotbart from the first attack, landing a strike with the tip of his sword to Rotbart's wrist precisely where the armor unlinked at the joint. Startled by the pain, Rotbart recoiled, but examining his wrist he found that, despite the blood, it was merely a surface wound. Hectored for his paltry performance by the knights watching from the slope, Rotbart pressed forward with renewed vigor. The battle now oscillated between the two fighters like two storm fronts swirling around each other—hurling and deflecting lightning bolts, towering above and rearing below the crack of heavy thunder. The square had been rid of its cobbles for the fight, and Friedrich now planted himself in the loose earth, shield and sword outstretched, until he was burrowed up to his spurs. There he parried deft blows to his head and chest from the small and nimble Rotbart, who seemed to engage from all sides at once. The battle had lasted nearly an hour when a new rash of jeering arose from the crowd—this time directed at Friedrich, whose entrenched defense was perceived as a refusal to counterattack Rotbart, whose own zealous ripostes were all too eager to bring the battle to a swift end. Although Friedrich's defense may have been steeped in strategy, he unfortunately allowed himself to be swayed by the crowd's heckling. He took a courageous step forward from the mounds forged around his spurs and delivered a series of lusty, forceful blows at the head of his opponent, who fended them off skillfully enough with his shield, though his strength was beginning to dwindle. Yet, just as the battle seemed to be changing course, Friedrich suffered a misstep, through which no higher power could have manifested itself—his foot became ensnared by his own spurs, and, stumbling onto his knees beneath the weight of his armor, he supported himself in the dust with one hand. Taking ignoble advantage of this compromising moment, Rotbart thrust his sword into Friedrich's exposed side. Friedrich sprang back with an anguished cry, but lowering his visor over his eyes, he turned back to face his opponent and continue the fight. But Friedrich's body bowed over in pain, and as he leaned on his sword, Rotbart stabbed him twice more, this time with his battle sword, in the chest beneath his heart. Friedrich collapsed to the ground in a clatter of armor, his sword and shield falling beside him. Rotbart tossed his weapons aside to the fanfare of trumpets, and placed a triumphant foot on Friedrich's chest. The Kaiser rose to his feet, and the crowds followed suit, to cries of horror and pity. Lady Helena rushed to her fallen son, writhing in the dust and blood, her daughters trailing close behind. "Oh, Friedrich!" She knelt at his head, wailing. Littegarde fainted and was lifted by two bailiffs and carried off, unconscious, to the castle's prison. "How dare she! That depraved woman put a sword in the hand of her most loyal friend knowing full well her own guilt—she used Friedrich's life to appeal to God's judgment in an unjust duel!" She cradled her beloved son's head in her hands and wept, while Friedrich's sisters freed him from his armor and frantically sought to stanch the blood from his chest. On the Kaiser's orders, however, the bailiffs came for Friedrich, too, placing him on a stretcher under doctors' care and carrying him off to the castle prison. Helena and her daughters were permitted to follow, and to remain at Friedrich's side until his death, which no one doubted was imminent.

It soon became evident, however, by some stroke of divine luck, that Friedrich's wounds, though affecting vital areas, were not fatal. In fact, within a few days the doctors were able to offer his mother and sisters no uncertain assurance that he would live. Given his robust constitution, they projected that he would recover within a matter of weeks, and his wounds would heal unscarred. No sooner had his senses returned that he began to ask after Littegarde. Friedrich could not contain his tears at the thought of Littegarde despairing in some abysmal prison cell, and he urged his sisters, stroking their chins tenderly, to visit and comfort her. His mother, however, was discomfited by this request, and she implored her son to forget such a scurrilous woman. Helena could pardon the crime that Rotbart had brought against Littegarde in court—which the duel's outcome had now confirmed—but she could not forgive the shameless impudence, with which Littegarde had nearly ruined her son by appealing for the divine verdict with a guilty conscience.

"But, Mother," Friedrich said, "no amount of wisdom could possibly make sense of the mysterious verdict which God intended through this duel."

"What? Do you not accept the obvious outcome of the duel? Did you not lie vanquished beneath your opponent's sword?"

"Yes, I may have momentarily succumbed, but I was not defeated. Was I seriously injured? Am I not still alive? Have I not recovered as though graced by heaven's very breath? Why, in a few days when my strength has doubled, or even tripled, I'll be ready to resume the fight that my own mere misstep prevented me from settling properly."

"Foolish boy, don't you know that a duel may not

be fought twice—not for the same purpose, not after a judge deems it settled, and certainly not to repeal God's verdict!"

"What use do I have for the arbitrary laws of men? If a duel hasn't been fought to the death of one of its combatants, how can it reasonably be considered settled? If only I were granted another chance, I would correct my misstep and use my sword to compel a wholly different verdict from God than that which you shortsightedly accept for fact."

"These laws which you claim to have no use for are nevertheless the measure by which we're all governed. Reasonable or not, they uphold divine authority—and you and Littegarde are now subject, like some insidious pair of criminals, to the strictest enforcement of that authority."

"That Littegarde should be judged guilty and condemned to death—and because of me!—it drives me to despair. In trying to prove her innocence, I've only brought misery upon her. One unsound step—God perhaps punishing my own heart's sins, not hers—and now her body is to be consumed by flames, her memory by eternal disgrace." Tears filled Friedrich's eyes, and he turned away, grasping for his handkerchief.

His mother and sisters knelt quietly at his bedside, pitying him with their own tears and kissing his hand. When the warden came to deliver his meal, Friedrich asked after Littegarde, and from the warden's terse, indifferent reply, Friedrich learned that she had lain on a bundle of straw in her cell and not spoken a word since the day of the duel. Worried for her well-being, he asked the warden to put her mind at ease by telling her how, by a miraculous stroke of luck, he was quickly recovering, and the warden willing, he would visit her in her cell as soon as he was strong enough. However, when the warden tried to convey the message, Littegarde stared blankly, making no indication of having heard. Fearing her mad, he shook her by the arm until finally she responded that she did not wish to see another human being the rest of her days on earth. That same day Littegarde wrote the warden a letter, instructing him not to grant anyone entrance to her cell—Sir Friedrich, most of all. Though thoroughly shaken by her refusal, Friedrich remained certain of her pardon, and on the first day that he was deemed strong enough to leave his cell, Friedrich, on the arms of his mother and sisters, went to pay a visit unannounced to Littegarde.

It was with indescribable dread, though, that Littegarde, at the sound of her cell door opening, rose from her straw bed with half-bared breast and unkempt hair and found Friedrich standing before her, her dear and loyal friend now pitiable and marked by suffering. "Go!" she cried, crumpling to the floor and desperately covering her face with her hands. "If there is even a glimmer of pity in your heart, then leave me!"

"Why, sweet Littegarde, why?" Friedrich stooped to her side, tenderly leaning over her and reaching for her hand.

"Please just go!" She cowered from his touch, crawling on her knees in the straw. "If you so much as touch me, I'll go mad! I'm horrified by you! Blistering flames terrify me less than you!"

"But Littegarde, it's me, *Friedrich*." He was devastated. "What have I done to deserve such treatment from you?" At a nod from his mother, his sister brought him a chair and helped him, weak as he was, onto it.

"Oh, God!" Littegarde threw herself at his feet, pressing her face to the ground in anguish. "Leave here, my beloved, and leave me. I beg of you— embracing your knee in passion, washing your feet with my tears, writhing like a worm in the dust—sir, lord, show me the mercy of leaving this room at once and abandoning me with it." Friedrich stood before her, shaken through and through.

"Is the sight of me truly so terrible, Littegarde?" he asked, looking down at her gravely.

"Horrible, unbearable, devastating—" She buried her face between his feet. "Hell with all its horrors is sweeter to face than your benevolent and loving countenance."

"Dear God, why do you do this to yourself? Has God's judgment revealed the truth—are you guilty of the crime that Rotbart brought before the court?"

"Guilty, convicted, judged, and condemned for eternity!" cried Littegarde, beating her breast. "God's truth is infallible. I've no more strength, not of mind nor of body. Go—leave me to my despair."

Friedrich fainted. His sisters rushed tearfully to his side to revive him. Littegarde drew a veil over her face and lay back down on her straw bed, as though she were taking leave of the world itself. "A curse upon you!" Helena cast at Littegarde. "A curse of eternal regret on this side of the grave and eternal damnation beyond—not for the deed which you now admit to, but for the ruthlessness and inhumanity which you only confess to now, after dragging my son into ruination with you. What a fool I've been." She turned her back on Littegarde. "If only I had listened to the Prior when, just before the duel began, he took me aside to disclose that Rotbart had gone to confession there at the Augustine monastery. In pious preparation for the decisive hour ahead of him, he swore on the holy host the truth of his testimony about this woman as he had revealed it before the court. Rotbart had described every detail: the garden gate where she had awaited him at nightfall; the uninhabited castle tower where she had led him, undetected by guards; the plush and plentiful pillows she had arranged beneath a canopy in the chamber where she secretly, shamelessly, bedded him. A solemn oath made at such an hour can contain no lies, and had I just warned my blinded son in those moments before the duel began, I could have opened his eyes and he would have retreated from the edge of that abyss. But come!" cried Helena, taking her son in her arms and kissing him on the forehead. "Protest will only dignify her words. May she shiver at our backs and despair at the punishment which we have spared her!"

"That wretched man!" Stung by Helena's words, Littegarde sat up and propped her head painfully upon her knee. Crying into her handkerchief, she said, "I remember that my brothers and I were at Rotbart's castle, three days before St. Remigius. He held a banquet in my honor, as he frequently took it upon himself to do. My father was flattered for a daughter of his to be paid such tribute, and persuaded me to accept the invitation at my brothers' accompaniment. That evening after the dancing at the banquet had ended, I found a note lying on the table in my room, written in an unknown hand and without a signature, containing a formal declaration of love. I was dumbfounded. My brothers had walked me to my door in order to discuss our departure the next day, and because I had never been one to keep a secret from them, I showed them the letter. They immediately recognized it as Rotbart's handwriting, and outraged, were prepared to march right into his room with letter in hand. But, as Rotbart had been shrewd enough not to sign the letter, confronting him seemed unwise. My brothers decided instead to set off that very night with me in our carriage and return to our father's castle, agreeing never again to privilege

Rotbart with our presence at any of his occasions. That," she declared, "is the only association I have ever had with that vile and despicable man."

"What?" said Friedrich, turning a tear-stained face toward Littegarde. "These words are music to my ears. Tell me again!" He knelt before her and folded his hands. "Have you not betrayed me with that miserable wretch? Are you pure of the guilt which he brought upon you before the court?"

"My dear," whispered Littegarde, pressing his hand to her lips.

"Are you?" Friedrich insisted. "Are you innocent?"

"As innocent as a newborn, as the conscience of a man fresh from confessional, as the body of a nun who died in the vestry while taking the veil."

"Oh, almighty God!" cried Sir Friedrich, hugging her around her knees. "Have thanks! Your words give me new life. Death no longer frightens me, and eternity, which just moments ago stretched before me like a sea of boundless misery, rises now with the brilliance of a thousand suns!"

"You poor man," said Littegarde, pulling away. "How can you believe a word of what I now say to you?"

"Why should I not?" asked Friedrich, glowing.

"Are you mad? Has God's holy judgment not decided against me? Did Rotbart not defeat you in that fateful duel? Has the accusation he brought against me in court not been vindicated through battle?"

"Oh, dearest Littegarde," cried Friedrich, "conserve your wits from despair! May the conviction within your heart spring up like a tower of rock that you may hold fast to and never waver, even if the earth should move beneath you and the heavens above you. Let us choose the kinder of the two thoughts which pervade our minds, and rather than believe yourself guilty, let us believe instead that because I fought for you, I will emerge as the true victor. God, Lord of my life," he said, covering his face with his hands, "guard my soul against confusion! Sure as I want my soul to be saved, I do not believe I suffered defeat by my opponent's sword. Although I was thrown to the dust beneath his heel, I have since risen. Why should divine wisdom proclaim its truth at only the very moment it is invoked? Oh, Littegarde," he said, taking her hand into his, "in life let us look to death and in death let us look to eternity, and throughout, let us hold firm to the belief that your innocence will be brought to the brilliant light of day through the duel that I have fought for you."The warden returned, and seeing Lady Helena weeping, reminded her that such stirrings of emotion could yet exhaust Friedrich in his convalescence. Friedrich allowed himself to be persuaded to leave Littegarde's side and return to his cell to rest, though not without the knowledge of having consoled and been consoled.

In the meantime, the charges against Sir Friedrich von Trota and Lady Littegarde von Auerstein were brought before the Kaiser's appointed court in Basel. Both were found guilty for having falsely invoked the divine verdict, and in accordance with the law, they were condemned to death and would be burned at the stake on the very field where the duel was fought. An envoy was sent to notify the prisoners, and the sentence would have been carried out immediately upon Sir Friedrich's recovery had it not been the Kaiser's intention that Count Jakob Rotbart—for whom he could not suppress his mistrust—be present at the execution. However, Rotbart himself had not yet recovered from the seemingly insignificant wound he had received from Friedrich at the very start of the duel. An unusual deteriorative condition prevented the wound from healing for days which then turned into weeks, and a procession of the most skilled doctors from Swabia and Switzerland proved unable to treat him. Indeed, some corrosive fluid, thoroughly unknown to the medicine of that time, had spread debilitating infection through his entire hand right down to the bone such that it had been necessary to amputate the hand—and, later, his arm, too, after the infection had continued to spread like a cancer. Even a treatment as radical as amputation could not prevent the infection from festering, and as Rotbart's body only deteriorated further, his doctors finally declared his condition untreatable and gave him but a week to live. The Prior from the Augustine monastery interpreted this sinister turn of events as an act of God and urged Rotbart to purge his conscience in his final days, but Rotbart took the holy sacrament once more, swearing on the truth of his testimony, and consigning his soul to eternal damnation if he should have falsely accused Littegarde.

Now, despite the dissolute life Rotbart had led up till this point, there was nonetheless reason to trust in his sincerity. The dying man possessed a piety that disallowed him from swearing a false oath at such a dire moment, and perhaps more importantly, the tower warden at Littegarde's father's castle, whom Rotbart claimed to have bribed in order to gain secret entrance on the night of St. Remigius, had corroborated his alibi upon formal questioning. This led the Prior to deduce that Rotbart himself must have been deceived by an unknown third party, and when Rotbart heard the news of Friedrich's miraculous recovery, he began to suspect as much himself.

It is important now to mention that before Rotbart had ever coveted Littegarde, he had been entangled in an illicit affair with her chambermaid, Rosalie. On nearly every one of Littegarde's visits to Rotbart's castle, he would lure the frivolous and wonton chambermaid to his room at night. Having neglected her of late, however, Rotbart succeeded only in stoking the chambermaid's envy with his letter, in which he declared his love for Littegarde. Although Rosalie accompanied Littegarde and her brothers on their hasty departure from Rotbart's castle that night, she surreptitiously left behind a letter for him signed in her Lady Littegarde's name, in which she explained that because his declaration of love had been perceived as an affront by her brothers, they would no longer be able to see each other publicly. On these grounds, she invited him to visit her at her father's castle on the night of St. Remigius. Rotbart was overjoyed and sent an immediate response announcing his certain arrival on the agreed-upon night, and in order to avoid notice, requested a trustworthy guide to lead him to her room. Experienced in the art of intrigue, Rosalie had been relying on such a reply, and sent a second duplicitous letter under the guise of her Lady, assuring Rotbart that she herself would be waiting at the garden gate in anticipation of his arrival. On the night before St. Remigius, Rosalie asked Littegarde for permission to take leave to the country, where her sister was ill and required attending, and she left the castle the very next afternoon with a bindle of linens under her arm, and, in full view of all the castle's staff, started off down the path in the direction of her sister's abode.

As night was beginning to fall, however, Rosalie returned to the castle under the pretext of a looming storm. She claimed to those who met her that she would continue her journey at the first light of day, and this being the case, she would simply have a bed prepared in a room within the castle's vacant tower so as not to disturb her Lady Littegarde. At midnight, Rotbart gained entrance to the castle by bribing the tower warden and was met by a veiled woman at the garden gate, whom he presumed to be Littegarde. The woman pressed a fleeting kiss on his mouth and led him up a staircase and to the entrance of a wing in which one of the most magnificent chambers in the entire castle lay, its windows shuttered in precaution. Taking him by the hand and whispering that her brothers' chambers were close by, she demanded silence as she lowered herself onto the bed with him. Rotbart was perfectly deceived by her form and figure, and he luxuriated in delirious pleasure to be making such a conquest at his age. At the first sign of the dawn's early light she dismissed him, placing a ring on his finger by which to remember their fleeting night, which Rosalie had removed from Littegarde's possessions earlier in the day. Rotbart promised her, as soon as he arrived back home to his castle, that he would reciprocate the gift by sending her a ring of his late wife's, which she had given to him on their wedding night. Three days later he kept his word, and Rosalie shrewdly intercepted the messenger, taking the ring back to the castle but keeping it in her secret possession. Rotbart was apprehensive about this adventure leading him too far astray, and thereafter he sent no further word and avoided any potential encounters with Littegarde. Rosalie was later expelled from the castle by Littegarde's brothers on the suspicion of theft and sent back to her parents' home on the Rhine, where over the course of the next nine months, the consequences of her own dissolute life became plainly visible. Her mother questioned her unrelentingly until she finally consented to naming Count Jakob Rotbart as the father of her child and confessed the elaborate scheme in which she had deceived him, producing his late wife's ring as evidence. Rosalie attempted to sell the ring, but its clear value found few buyers who could afford it, and indeed, it even raised a few suspicions as to how a woman like Rosalie had procured such a ring. The truth of the girl's testimony could not be brought into doubt with the ring as evidence, however, and her parents thus proceeded to bring a lawsuit against Rotbart over the custodial support of his child. The court appointed to hear their suit was well aware of the trial currently preoccupying all of Swabia and

Switzerland, and their discovery of new information pertaining to Count Jakob Rotbart was to be rushed to Basel, as it bore importance to the trial's outcome. A councilman headed to Basel on business was to personally deliver the letter containing Rosalie's testimony as well as Rotbart's ring, with the hope of delivering a solution to this terrible puzzle.

On the day that Sir Friedrich and Lady Littegarde were to be executed—which the Kaiser, unaware of the doubts newly riddling Rotbart's mind, decided could not be postponed a day longer—the councilman delivered Rosalie's testimony to Rotbart. The dying man was in great discomfort, shifting painfully in his bed, when the councilman arrived. After reading the letter and examining the ring, Rotbart called once again for the Prior. "Enough! The sun casts too kind a light on a wretch like me. Take me to the execution so that I may perform one just deed before I die." The Prior was moved by Rotbart's contrite lastrequest and had four servants lift him onto a stretcher and carry him back to the square where the duel had been fought. They arrived amid tolling bells and made their way through the immense crowd to where Friedrich and Littegarde were bound to the stake.

"Stop!" shouted the Prior, as Rotbart was set down below the Kaiser's balcony. "Before that pyre should be lit, this sinner has a confession."

"What?" The Kaiser stood, pale as a corpse. "Did the divine verdict not uphold his cause? After all that has transpired, how can Littegarde possibly be innocent of the sin this very man accused her of?" Astounded, the Kaiser stepped down from his balcony, and an immense crowd including more than a thousand knights followed suit, abandoning the benches and platforms to gather around the dying man.

"Innocent!" Rotbart, clutching a crucifix in his hand, sat up with the Prior's help. "The almighty God handed down a verdict of innocence before all the eyes of Basel on that fateful day. Despite receiving three seemingly mortal wounds, Sir Friedrich now thrives, fully recovered in strength and vigor, whereas a mere scratch from the tip of his sword has felled me as a storm does an oak, worming its way to the core of my being. To extinguish any remaining doubt, such is the truth: it was Lady Littegarde's chambermaid, Rosalie, who received me on the night of St. Remigius while I, deceived by my own senses, thought it was Littegarde herself whom I held in my arms—Littegarde, who has always spurned my every advance."

The Kaiser stood a moment, still as stone, before turning to the pyre and ordering a knight to climb the ladder, untie Sir Friedrich and Lady Littegarde, and bring them to him. "An angel must surely watch over every hair on your head," the Kaiser pronounced, as Littegarde approached. Disheveled and with half-bared breast, she leaned on Friedrich, whose own steps trembled from the miraculous redemption. The crowds parted for them in awe and wonder. They knelt before the Kaiser, and he kissed them both on the forehead. The Kaiser asked his wife for her ermine cloak and draped it around Littegarde's shoulders, while Friedrich was given a plumed hat and knight's mantle for his condemned man's shirt. There in the presence of all the chivalry, the Kaiser took Littegarde's arm to personally escort her into the palace. He paused a moment, though, and, turning compassionately back to Rotbart, who writhed pitiably on his stretcher, asked a doctor standing by whether there was any hope for the dying man, who had, after all, taken up the gauntlet in good faith.

"None," replied Rotbart, amid painful convulsions. "However, my death is deserved. As I am well beyond the reach of mortal law now, I confess that I am the murderer of my brother, the honorable Duke Wilhelm von Breysach. Six weeks ago, I hired the assassin who struck my brother dead with an arrow from my own armory—all to reap the crown for myself." Rotbart fell back onto the ground, his blackened soul leaving his body.

The Duchess Katharina had followed the Kaiser and his wife down to the square to hear Rotbart's dying confession. "Why, it's just as my husband had suspected! With his last breaths, he uttered as much, but I could scarcely comprehend it at the time."

Indignantly, the Kaiser declared: "If not his soul, then at least his corpse shall be seized by the arm of justice. Bailiffs, take him! Treat him as a convicted man, and turn him over to the executioner. Brand his memory in eternal disgrace on the same pyre where two innocent souls nearly perished for his sins."

While Rotbart's wretched corpse crackled in the red flames and the north wind blew his ashes to the lengths of the land, the Kaiser and all his knights escorted Lady Littegarde into the palace. By the

Kaiser's decree, Littegarde's inheritance from her father—which her brothers in their avarice had already seized—was fully restored to her. Three weeks later, at the castle in Breysach, the noble couple celebrated their marriage, at which the Duchess, delighted by the turn in events, made a wedding gift to Littegarde of Rotbart's forfeited estates, and the Kaiser laid a medal of bravery around Friedrich's neck. Upon his return to Worms he had the statutes governing divine trial by duel amended to state that the revelation of guilt shall not be immediately presumed "...unless it be God's will."

THIS IS A MELVILLE HOUSE ▣HYBRIDBOOK

HybridBooks are a union of print and electronic media designed to provide a unique reading experience by offering additional curated material—**Illuminations**—which expand the world of the book through text and illustrations.

Scan the code or follow the link below to gain access to Illuminations for *The Duel* by Heinrich von Kleist, including writings by:

Paul the Deacon • J.G. Millingen • Sir Walter Scott • Johann Ludwig Uhland • Miguel de Cervantes • Andrew Lang • John Carl Blankenagel And the twelve laws of chivalry

As an added bonus, each book in The Duel series contains a "Duelist's Supplement," a fascinating compendium on the art, history and literature of dueling.

The Duel by **Giacomo Casanova** contains "Duels, Duelists and Dueling Grounds: A Survey of the Infamous and Bizarre"

The Duel by **Anton Chekhov** contains "Against the Duel: Writing in Protest of Dueling"

The Duel by **Joseph Conrad** contains "The Code Duello: A Diverse Anthology for Personal Use"

The Duel by **Heinrich von Kleist** contains "The Art of Dueling: How to Shoot and Slash Your Way to Satisfaction"

The Duel by **Alexander Kuprin** contains "The Other Duel: Fiction and Poetry Concerning Duels"

Download a QR code reader in your smartphone's app store, or visit mhpbooks.com/kleist518